All proceeds from the sale of this book
will be donated to
St. Jude Children's
Research Hospital

in honor of
Elena Martinez
who was triumphant over leukemia.

Thinkin' about Stuff

by

Terry Focht

Illustrated by
Rachel Boyer

Illustrated by Rachel Boyer

Printed in the United States of America

First Printing, 2023

ISBN 978-1-955791-68-7

For questions or comments about this book, please write to info@braughlerbooks.com.

This book is dedicated to

Bob Miranda

Bob Brown

Jessee Begley

And to the loving memory of

Craig Wulfeck Sr.
(1945-2023)

The most fun and funniest
Best Friends a person could ever have

Rottenreads
Rates this book as

IMMATURE

On all levels

You are about to read
a book by

Terry Focht

God Knows Why!

If you begin to shake
uncontrollably or run
around in circles, please
seek medical attention
immediately!

From the
Award-Winning Author

Terry Focht

Winner of the 5th grade 100-yard dash

Winner of the 7th grade fast dance
contest

Winner of the 8th grade splellinng
contest

3 Time Winner
*** The Delbert Award ***
for
Rookie of the Year

Special Award
Worlds Best Grandfather
It says so on his coffee cup

About the Illustrator

It is with great pleasure that the author introduces **Rachel Boyer,** a talented young artist and creative to the literary community.

Rachel and Terry were brought together by Sherry Cook Stanforth, Founder/Director, Originary Arts Initiative through their participation in the Place Keepers Forum, a vital part of the Originary Arts Initiative.

Rachel Boyer is a Digital artist and Illustrator who graduated with a BFA from Thomas More University. Rachel has worked with everything from paper and canvas to digital media to create an expression filled aesthetic to her works. She is an artist that finds inspiration from all aspects of life but mostly her great love of flowers. She desires every one of her art pieces to display an expression of love and joy, just as flowers do for her.

About the Author

Terry Focht, is not what you would call an intellectual writer. **Really**, he isn't. Seriously, believe me he is *definitely* not.

He seems to get great joy in massacring both poetry and prose in a way so baffling,
you have to scratch your head or someone else's head if you prefer.

With previous works like: Grandpa Toots, Chicken Butts, Pineapple Upside Down Head, Belly Button Ballet and Princess Tooty Pants, you start to get the picture of a very goofy man, weird, that's right whacko.

He tries to take the reader to places inside his brain, like the place where a little boy spread jelly all over his body and topped it with peanut butter, or His Head's Too Big for his Britches, or a Dinosaur Convention. He writes about a frog named Shelly that slept alone in the alley and wore some spectacles just to look respectables.

By the way while you're in there, in his brain, that is, Terry asks that before you leave, that you please sweep away the cobwebs and maybe dust a bit. Oh yeah, be sure to turn out the light when you leave.

Terry loves to bring us face to face with toots, belly buttons, jelly up your nose, life as a worm, tie dyeing belly button lint, armpit music and what it's like to be old.
Be careful, because he sometimes likes to play tricks on the readers.

Terry's first book "I Was an Only Child" really pissed off his sister.

He is sarcastic enough to show up at local literary events, invited or not.

I highly recommend you run away **right now** Run and never look back in case there is **any chance** he might influence you in any way. And if your name happens to be Forrest then "Run Forrest Run."

Terry claims to have invented handles.
He also claims to have invented verbal shorthand, pickles, burps and snickerdoodles.

We really like snickerdoodles! Does anyone have any extra snickerdoodles? If you do…I can almost guarantee you a part of the cast if this book ever gets to Hollywood and for 2 snickerdoodles I will promise you a part if it gets to Broadway.

Table of Contents

To Heck with the Table of Contents

Every dagone book you pick up
has a Table of Contents.

Try this magical formula for reading
instead.
1. Open Book
2. Read the first page
3. Turn to the next page
4. Read until you get to the end

Say it with me now---
To heck with the Table of Contents.

Wait just a minute now!

Maybe I spoke to hastily. **I may have changed my mind.**
I can't miss such a great opportunity to honor people I love in a non-traditional way.

Maybe instead of page numbers – **I will name the pages.**
Maybe I will name the pages with my favorite people I love or names that I just love, or cake or pie. Yumm!

If I forget to include your name – do not be offended.
I probably just forgot.

Or *maybe* I don't love you as much as you thought I did.

The Page Number/Page Name Quandary

Because of Terry's love for the reader, Terry has decided to offer you co-authorship of his book by allowing the reader to number or name the pages, of his or her, own private book.

After extensive research at the Library of Congress, Harvard, Yale, Princeton, MIT, Stanford and Belmont High School in Dayton Ohio, it appears this has never been done before in all of history. Wow, what an honor for you!

How's that for a gift from the author? You are now participants in a profound piece of literature, sure to become compared with all the other sacred documents of our country.

As a totally unbiased typist I would say it belongs up there with the great religious writings as well.

So now all you have to do is put the page numbers down in the right-hand corner of each page or if you choose to name the pages instead feel free to put the names anywhere you choose.

Remember though, this is a family book so please keep it clean.

On behalf of the parents of children who read this book under the age of 14 we ask that you also keep your shirts and shoes on while reading. Well except for Matthew McConaughey, we know how difficult that is for him.

The Secret Word

It has come to my attention that because this book contains many of the **secrets of life**, that books like this should have a **Secret Word.**

Now that I understand this, I want to do a little research first before I reveal the **Secret Word.** You know, stuff I need to be concerned about like copyright infringements, patents, the Bible, etc.

Should it perhaps be written in code? Do I need to register the word with the Library of Commerce or the Secret Service? I wonder if that is what they do in the Secret Service. I will call them today and find out. **This is just that urgent**! Or, maybe I'll do it tomorrow, or the next day.

You will hear from me later on in this book about the progress of the **Secret Word,** but for now keep this to yourself. I don't want to alert spies from other countries that might try to steal this important piece of intellectual property.

Remember---don't tell anybody!
Or, No one either!
Or anyone!
Or, nobody!

Well, you **can** tell Dr. Sherry Cook-Stanforth. We can trust her.
Just remind her that she shouldn't write a song about it.

Remember Now
It's a secret!!

Secrets are essential to the security of our country.
So please, no tellin'...

I know all about secrets.

I was once a Secret Agent.

Oops!

I wasn't supposed to tell you that!
That was supposed to be a secret also.
So, shhh!

I hope you can keep 2 secrets.

The
Reader's Page,

Hey you!
That's right you.

This is your page.
You can write, scribble,
draw or doodle on this page.

Because this is your page
and nobody else's.

This page too!

Go ahead doodle away.
You earned it.

All you readers have been
waiting so long to be
acknowledged.

You are now among the
very first
to receive
**Reader's Page
Recognition.**

You can now doodle
to your heart's content.

Secrets for the Intellectual Reader

Hey! --- (I said Intellectual)
Who do you think your kidding?

The following secrets are the answer to all your problems and two of your neighbors across the street. Be absolutely sure to not lend this book to them. Make them buy their own.
The author has no hidden agenda here. Well maybe it's a little hidden.

Official additional Secret reading directions:

1. Look at pages.
2. Read 'em all.
3. Try to look serious, tap the side of your head.
4. Look at the ceiling and say hmm.
5. Hum if you like. But, not to Sweet Georgia Brown, or your liable to start dribbling between your legs, or passing behind your back.

6. If you must, feel free to purr, buzz or vibrate if it makes you feel good.
7. Do not whirr however. Whatever you do – **do not** whirr!
Again – Do Not Whirr.
Consider this a warning!

Some free extra advice
Never start a sentence with Oops.
Especially do not say Oops,
if you are writing for poets.
Personally, I am afraid of poets
and heights.
Especially Poet Laureates in tall
buildings.
They are really scary!

If I Were a Frog

If I were a frog named Shelly
That slept alone in the alley

I'd sleep with one eye open
To keep from getting broken

I'd hide from the man
As best as I can

'Cause that scary ole man
With those huge stinky feet

That ugly old man
Might step on me

I'd drink a little whiskey
And more than a little beer

Than croak out my song
For all to hear

I'd befriend a scruffy mouse
And a tomcat too

I might even be friends with you
If you asked me to

I'd wear some spectacles
Just to look respectables

I'd lay my head
In a shoe for a bed

I'd cover my body
Not to tempt...anybody

"Cause I sleep every night
Alone in the alley

I'd hide from the cats
The dogs and the hogs

And hope they won't see
What a yummy meal I might be

Chicken Butts

My four-year-old granddaughter
Informed her mom this day

A girl from her school had
Chicken butts
She hopes they go away

Her mommy told her not to worry
She already had her shots

I'm sure you won't get
Chicken Butts

You silly little nut

Mommy got you all your shots
Every shot you need
& all the mommies are very thankful
For the *Chicken Butts* vaccine

Attention Chicken Butts Lovers

Larry the Cable Guy was right.
That Chicken Butts story is funny!
That there Chicken Butts is funny right there.
I don't care who you are.
Well unless maybe you're the chicken.

Chicken Butts and a couple other pieces, were stolen
from

Grandpa Street

You know the one on Amazon for only $12.95.
Wow, What a deal!!!

Legal Notice

*** Grandpa Street ***

Was written by the same author – **Me.**
I didn't actually ask permission from myself,
I hope I don't have to sue myself for copyright
infringements.

Hear Ye – Hear Ye

This book
Forever Known as

Thinkin' about Stuff

As of July 4th 2023
This Day of the Lord

Hereby and forthwith

Bans Boston
Beans and All

Icky Sticky Fun

Little Billy told me
About his dream last night
He dreamed a funny story
Full of funny sounds
Like beans and feets
Clowns and frowns

He dreamed
He got him a big ole jar of jelly
Stuck in his finger and rubbed it on his belly
He licked that finger...that he dipped in the jelly
Before it got too icky
Too sticky or too smelly

It felt so good and he knew that he could
So he took that jar and he dropped to the floor
And rubbed that jelly on his feet and more

He rubbed it on his ankles and on his toes
On his ears and his lobes
And the tip of his nose

He rubbed it on his shirt
And on his buttons
Rubbed it on his tummy
And his belly button

He *got* him some bread
For his body full of jelly
And plopped him some peanut butter
Smack dab on his belly

Bread and peanut butter
Peanut butter and jelly
Really good for eatin'
Great for actin' silly

PB&J
On his feets and his toes
His Adam and his apple
His belly and his button
His ears and his lobes
His El and his Bows
And just a tiny little
Just a teeny, tiny little
Up his nose

Old Friends

We sit
We commiserate
Enjoy old stories
Retell old lies

Most of all we sit
My friends and I

Critical, Crucial and Kinda' Important!

Never use the justify symbol,
even when it is justified.

There is just
No justification for it.

Thinkin' about Stuff

Sometimes I rest my head on my fist and think about stuff.
I call those times…**Thinkin' about Stuff.**

Stuff like the following:

Good News At The Funeral Home
I saw a beautiful cherry casket
I wasn't in it

The Secret of a Long Marriage
Always say "**Yes Dear**"
and you'll always be right.

The Secret of a Long Marriage – Part 2
Start each day by boldly saying – **I'm Sorry!**

I knew I Found Miss Right
I did not know her first name was – Always.

The Worst Things About Politics
Politicians

A Precious Gift
Upon retiring, I received a most precious gift.
A gift so rare that it took my breath away.
I have never been more grateful for such a
wonderful, ongoing gift:
Naps.

Thank You Lord!
I needed to go to the bathroom
Everything worked

The next one is the most important thing I ever
wrote
I call it...
The Most Important Thing I Ever Wrote
Cancer tried to destroy me.
It failed...
Let's Eat!

**Good by for now, it's the middle of the day and
the sun is
shining brightly, people are at work, and it's time
for my nap.**

Pineapple Upside Down Head

If I had a head made out of pineapple
I would plop it down on top of a cake
& stand on my head
'Til it was time for bed

But in the morning when it was time to awake
My head would have a *bellyache*

This kind of stuff happens
When you stand on your head
Upside down
'Til you go to bed

'Til your face gets red
'Til your belly gets a headache
'Cause you stood to long
On top of a cake

My Heads Too Big For My Britches

In the land of inside out and upside down
I bumped my head while falling down
And when I woke up in my bed
A great green monster was in my head
He was green and blue
And smelled like a shoe

A smelly ole monster
With a big fat head

When that monster woke
He jumped out of bed
Then that big ole ugly
Kicked me in the head

Now once awake
It was time to dress
To think things over
And get out of this mess

I grabbed my shirt
And tied it to my toe
Put my shoes
On my nose
But it was hard to blow
I took my britches
And tried to step in 'em
I pushed and I pushed
But couldn't get in 'em

So, I put those britches up on my head
I pulled, pulled and pulled
But just couldn't pull 'em down

I looked in the mirror
And began to frown
'Cause that big ole monster
On my shoulders I found

A big ugly monster
A smelly ole mess
With an empty wine bottle
Beside my bed

I asked that mirror
Could it be?
Could that big smelly monster
Really be me?

Terry loves to jibber-jabber

So if you're up for a little jibber-jabber, this is the place to be.

However, before you are granted jibber-jabber privilege for reading this book,
you must first submit a formal request for a **Free Style Jibber-Jabbering License** from the **Department of Jibber-Jabber**, headquartered and manned by U.S. Congress members in Washington D.C. when they are not busy.
So, anytime between 8am to 11pm Monday through Sunday is fine.

Note---Congress lunches daily between 11am to 3pm.
In addition---their half hour break times are at the top of the hour, every hour.

We have it from a very legitimate source that Congress is rich with first-class
"Olympic Level," Jibber-Jabberers. Many are Olympic Level, Gold Medal,
Marathon Jibber–Jabberers.

This license is valid throughout the United States and may also be used as a
Fishing License, in the states of Ohio and Kentucky.

Special Note---Ohio is very health conscious, so if you normally fish with dough balls for bait be sure to only use Gluten-Free Dough balls in Ohio's lakes, Rivers and Streams. There has been a rise in Gluten allergies for Large Mouth Bass and Catfish.

For Jibber-Jabber scholarships, you must be recommended by a
Licensed, Marathon Level, Jibber-Jabberer Congressman.
All congressmen fit the criteria.

Attention Readers

Terry would really love to see your best picture of you or a puppy making funny faces here, BETWEEN THESE LINE, PLEASE.

So if you would like to contribute your pictures and if you can find out where to send them to, please do so by the 4th of July, 2023.

Terry's Favorite Word is **Indubitably**
He likes to see it in all capital letters, in
the middle of the page,
in bold print and italicized.

INDUBITABLY

Wish I Could Go Fishin'

Wish I could go fishin'
At early morning light
Fishin' in the daytime
Fishin' late at night

But fishin's not for me, they say
'Cause I'm getting kinda old

Guess it wasn't meant to be
Or so I've been told

But wait just a minute now

Grandpa's got another idea, you see
'Cause
You're never too old to go fishin'
If it's where you want to be

What It's Like To Be Old

I'll tell you what it's like to be old
It's harder to touch your toes

Harder to get up
Harder to go
Gotta be careful
When you blow your nose

It's much too easy to take a nap
Harder to scratch your very own back

It's harder to lift
Harder to sit

Gotta' be sure to wear a hat

It's harder to reach
All the places you need

Harder to get around
Harder to get to the ground

Gotta' be careful
When you try to lean over
For fear of falling into the clover

You even have to limit your snacks...
You even have to limit your snacks...
You even have to limit your snacks...
Can you imagine that?

Grandpa Street

Here I sit on Grandpa Street
Reclined but not asleep

I watch the news
And political shows

Oh dear Lord
I wish I was asleep

I'm Still Not Done

Silver or white
Gray or bald

Like it or not
We all get old

A little more cranky
A lot more creaky

Gee I wish
I could oil my bones

Too much tummy
Not much fun

Flabby but happy
'Cause I'm still not done

Intermission

**Wine and cheese and
fancy desserts
will be served in the lobby.**

If it's good enough for Broadway
It's good enough for us.

Tiramisu – Beignets – Cream Éclairs
Chocolate Raspberry Cheesecake

Secret Word Update

Well folks, thanks for your patience!
It has been a long wait and the **Secret Word** Application is now awaiting final approval from the Department of Secrets, somewhere in Washington D.C. The location of the Department of Secrets is such a secret, you have to be put on a secret waiting list before they can even let you know their secret address. Then in 11 days, you can go to the Department of Secrets, to pick up your official government approved, Secret Word application by the Department of Secrets. Until then, your Secret Word and the address of the Department of Secrets is a strict secret.

So in just 7 & 11/12s more days I will be able to reveal the much-anticipated **Secret Word** of this book. Then, you too will be made a recipient of many of the secrets of life.

The magical day will be here soon and you have my word that the Secret Word will be revealed on the last page of this book, but you must keep that a secret too. Or, oh boy, will we all be in trouble then.

Trouble I say, trouble, trouble, trouble. (Remember that guy from the movie 42?) quite a dramatic scene, I thought.

Raise your right hand and say I promise.

Remember now... "_you promised_"

Those Crazy Dinosaurs

Just a short while ago
66 million years and not much more
The annual Dinosaur Convention
Was about to take place
To discuss the topic
Of climate change

The meeting wouldn't take very long
You see
Because *those crazy ole dinosaurs*
Didn't believe

They were so busy eating
Their meats and their greens
Or roaring at others
Their disproven beliefs

All was thought fine
Until one day
They began to believe
Just a little too late

They all massed together
In fear of being baked
Crying to their leader
Wishing, hoping
Praying to be saved

Their outrageous leader
Defiantly
Raised his bright orange head
Shaking his tiny little fists
As the asteroids landed

Volcanoes erupted
Tsunamis grew
Ashes towered to the heavens

And in one last stand
The crazy ass leader
Squared his shoulders
Lifted his burnt orange chin
And roared at the heavens

One last time...*Fake News*

Grandpa's Socks

Pull your socks up grandpa
Before you take me to the park

They're so white and pretty
You don't want to get them dirty

Pull your socks up grandpa
Because they're getting really wrinkly

Kinda loose and squiggly
A little old and stinky

Hold on kiddo
I think you outht'a know

I'm not wearing any socks

So come on
If you want to go

Hey!

You Again?

Am I Hearing Things?
Am I Hearing Things?

Are you still Whirring?

I didn't think so.

Discipline

My teacher told me
I had an attention problem
Monkeys like to fart

I know three people who like toes

My teacher said
I must learn to discipline my mind
To pay attention in class

I can eat a candy bar twice as fast as a monkey

My teacher said that I was doing better
I was sorry to hear that I was sick

Maybe I'll send myself a card

Grandpas Secret Dream

I wish I had a bicycle
I could ride around my street

A bright and shiny bicycle
I could ride for weeks and weeks

A bicycle of many colors
Red and yellow, blue and green

A bicycle to love forever
To ride on
In my dreams

I wish I wasn't too old
To have a bicycle for a friend

To ride around in circles
'Til it's time to go to bed

A cute and funny bicycle
My very bestest friend

And in my dream

My favorite
Favorite dream

I would name
My funny bicycle

Mr. Jelly Bean

Didn't you hear me?

I said do not whirr!!!

Did you bump your head?

Are you new?

This is your last chance---

Do
Not
Whirr

Please, it is for your own good.

My Oughtobiography

I don't exercise enough but I oughto

I'm gonna try a little harder or I oughto

I oughto watch my weight but it's hard to

I oughto quit eating so many donuts but I'm not gonna'

I oughto go on a diet but I don't buy it

I oughto try to be a little nicer or I oughto

I oughto quit watching so much TV but It wouldn't be me

You oughto go to a movie with me if y'anto

I oughto work a little harder but I don't want to

I oughto quit making lists of oughto's or I oughto

I wish this list could be more funny or it oughto

To fill out the rest of this page:
I oughto put a big picture of a hippopotamus in a pink tutu

Or...
an alligator with sunglasses on

Or...

a picture of Terry looking at things backward, upside down between his legs, you know... like he was running for President of the United States

Well... *actually*, you can fill out the page by
just playing with the spacing, bold type and font size.
Let this be a lesson to you!

Or, you oughto!

Can **you** think of anything that you would like to see
right here?
Go ahead, you can do it. I have confidence in you!
You really oughto, if y'anto

Let's Eat Fungus

I remember the day
When the mushrooms ran away

They ran through the woods
To join the land

To a beautiful forest
A new place...to expand

Where their aunts were toads
And their uncle's stools
And so many cousins
They could not fool

They hid in the ground
And fooled around

Swallowed the earth and
Gave new birth

Black and gray
White and brown

Beautifully blended fungi
What a beautiful sound

They were gathered and adored
And brought to the store

The tastiest of treats
$2.00 a pound...
and not much more.

No Worries

When I was young I worried
I worried about getting old

Worried about
What I might not be able to do

My favorite things
I do with you

I worried about forgetting
The things that brought me to now

But since I got old
I don't worry any more

I wouldn't remember anyhow

Grandpa Snores

I cannot sleep when Grandpa snores
He snores and snores
Then he snores some more

I'd like to sit on Grandpa's lap
It's the perfect place to take a nap

He has a big belly
All soft like jelly

I'd like to cuddle him
But I can't

'Cause he snores so loud
He sounds like a crowd

He's just too loud
To take my nap

Secret Word Final Update

Well folks, I gotta' tell ya', I am very disappointed!

It appears one of the secret rules from the **Department of Secrets** is that they must keep your **Secret Word** a **Secret** until the book has reached a million copies sold.

So, you all have my sincere apologies. I will be unable to share with you the secrets of life until the stupid **Department of Secrets** criteria has been met.

So for now you will just have to encourage everyone including yourself to buy multiple copies of this book until it has reached the high standards of secrecy and I then will be able to reveal the secrets of life to my legions of loyal fans.

Until then I guess the **Secret Word** is a **secret.**
At least that's what the **Department of Secrets say.**

* That is the last time I will tell the Department of Secrets any secrets of mine.

Terry's Favorite Restaurant Names

Toots

Burgers and Burps

Hamburgers and Hiccups

Exlax , Burgers to Go   (my favorite)

Weiner World

Whiskey, Wieners and Whatchmacallits

Joes Bar and Grill and Bar

Why Wait, Eat Now, Go Later

Gurgling Gertrudes

First Church of the Corn Dog

Benedict Botulisms

Lillian Lardbottoms

Scrumptious Gas

Fantastic Flab

Good God Goodhearts

Stinky Eats

Corn Dog Deli

Dyslexic Hot Gods

Toots Vegetarian Cuisine

Eats Toots and Booze

Grandpas, a Place to Burp Outloud

Arm Farts Dinner Theatre

Whoopee for the Weiner

Gas To Go

Gaseous Rumblings

Oops Excuse Me

Oops I Gotta Go

Big Weiners

Real Big Wieners

Bigger Wieners
Really, Really, Big Wieners
Excuse Me I am so Embarrassed
Ah, That Feels Better
Sorry We Can't Help It
Don't Ever Do That Again
Food that Squeaks

My Aching Back and Feet

I gotta' be active
I gotta' go
If I wanna' stay on my toes

Not as easy as I thought it would be
Now that I'm getting old

I'm out of my recliner
And into my soles
My back's a little bent
But I'm ready to roll

Come on feet, come on toes
You gotta' get going
You gotta' go
I gotta' move...those feets and toes

Easy Street

Excuse me kind sir
Could you please direct me
To Easy Street

I've looked and I've looked
Forever and a year

Maybe, just maybe
I'll find it here

I've asked for directions
I've asked if it's near

To my right or my left
To the front or the rear

I thought it might be there
I hoped it might be here

But, as I grow weary
I'm beginning to think

Maybe, just maybe

It might not
Be anywhere

Grandpa's Recliner

My recliner is a special place
A special place to think
But I've got to do it quick, you see
Before I start to blink

'Cause when I lay back all the way
When my feet are pointed west

Before I know it
It soon becomes

My favorite place to rest

The End

I finished this book today
My wife made
A fancy meal
To celebrate

Every bite
Fit into my mouth,
Perfectly.

Turn to the next page right now!

Go ahead ...

I Dare You!

Fooled you!

This is the real The End.

Well maybe there might be just 1 more
The End.

Who knows it may come at any time in
this book

Or,
Maybe, just maybe it might come in
my next book

Or,
Who knows, maybe it will be in
your book.

The End #3

Wait just a minute you say.
How many 'The Ends' do you need?

It's like the author doesn't have any respect for the
rules.

Or,
Structure
Form
Punctuation
Page Numbers
Bold Print
Italics
Italicized Bold Print
Splleling
The rules of English
The rules of Publishing

And how about that Table of Contents page?
Are you kidding me?

Who wrote this thing anyway?

What!
Terry Focht wrote it!
Well that explains it.

Well at least there were some great illustrations by
Rachel Boyer.

Bonus Page

Top Secret stuff about the author found in the restroom of an ex-President.

You must not read this unless you have a Security Clearance.

The stuff was marked Top Secret, that's how we know that it was Top Secret. However the ex-President denied ever knowing the author who wrote this crap and refused to even make up a lie about him. Which was **extremely rare** for the ex-President. He thought Terry was just that inconsequential.

This is the story of a retired educational professional that upon retirement had a difficult decision to make...and the story goes something like this.

Upon retirement this rustbelt wonder did not know what he was going to do with himself. Terry had narrowed his choices down to Movie Star, Rock Legend, Broadway Dancer, Tap Dancing Yodeler or Famous Writer.

After much consideration Terry decided to become a famous writer but for reasons you might not think. It was more of a practical decision you see. He already had a pen and it was very light, so it was doubtful he would rupture anything. He had been the 8th grade spelling bee champion after all. He had a notebook and some paper, a recliner with 10 positions, so his decision became very easy.

Terry has never regretted that decision and now dreams of things like the Pulitzer, the Nobel Prize, the Delbert and maybe, does he dare to say it, Readers Digest.
Most of all Terry prides himself for making such a wise choice.

Think about it, have you ever lifted a pen?
There are virtually no recorded hernias attributed to pen lifting.

Praise for Terry's Book

Terry's masterful delusionary insight into the writing world is truly a remarkable piece of jibberish that will leave you begging for less.

***Kerry Tarvin*, a Reader's Digest Subscriber**

This effort of Terry Focht is an instant classic of the genre...good enough to be the capstone of a semi-mediocre writing career. Let's hope it is the last from Terry Focht.

***Alex Martinez*, an expert on corn.**
The vegetable not this book.

Terry's lyrical voice will draw comparisons to Hemmingway. It is that seductive,
I could not put it down. I could not believe what I was reading. Extraordinary!

***Ed*, at the Dairy Queen**

Terry Focht has examined his ferocious brain, walked around in it, relived it, and with the skill and care and generosity of heart, has generated it into a triumphant work of nonsense. This book is destined to be on everyone's list of books you forget to read. It is a masterpiece of nonsense, drivel and jibberish.

Jessee Begley, who spent a lot of time staring out his window at Belmont Park. *Co-Author of "H is for Harvard, Ain't That Swell."

What a great sensation. It was like having a lemon, a dill pickle and sour milk in your mouth at the same time, only to be relieved by spitting it out. My bowels were moved.

Bob Miranda, who lives in the land of tulips but does not wear wooden shoes often.

Wow! Are you kidding me? This has to be a joke. Right? Did he bump his head?

Pastor Bob Brown, the winner of the U.S. Grant 7th Grade, Hop Skip and Jump Contest